Back Off, Bully Boys!

by Kitty Richards
illustrated by Bob Ostrom

SCHOLASTIC INC.
New York Toronto London Auckland Sydney
Mexico City New Delhi Hong Kong Buenos Aires

**KLASKY
CSUPO**INC.

Based on the TV series *Rugrats*® created by Arlene Klasky, Gabor Csupo, and
Paul Germain as seen on Nickelodeon®

ISBN 0-439-66679-1

12 11 10 9 8 7 6 5 4 3 2 1   4 5 6 7 8 9/0

Printed in the U.S.A.

First Scholastic printing, September 2004

Angelica stood at the very top of the monkey bars looking out over the playground. Everyone was digging in the sandbox looking for the treasure she had told them was buried there. Angelica smiled a satisfied smile. She was in charge.

Tommy came running over. "We didn't find any treasure, Angelica," he reported.

"I was hopin' it was a treasure chest full of gummy worms," said Lil sadly. Then she brightened, reaching into her pocket. "But I did find this lollipop!" She held up the sand-encrusted sucker proudly.

"I saw it first, *Lillian*," Phil said.

"I don't think so, *Phillip*," said Lil.

"Forget about the lollipop, silly babies," Angelica said with an exasperated sigh. "It's got sand all over it. Let's play another game." "How about one we never played before?" Tommy suggested.

"We're going to play the 'I Dare You' game!" Angelica said. "We all make up dares for each other to do!"

"Me first! Me first!" said Phil. He pointed to Tommy's dog, who was sleeping under a park bench. "I dare Tommy to . . . kiss Spike!"

"That's easy!" said Tommy. He ran over and gave his dog a big smooch.

Lil looked at Kimi. "I dare Kimi to act like a . . . monkey!"

Kimi jumped up and down, and made funny "ooh-ooh-ooh" noises.

Everyone laughed.

"I dare Lil to . . . eat a bug!" Chuckie chimed in.

Lil rolled her eyes. "Chuckie, I already eated three!"

"Can't any of you dumb babies come up with a really good dare?" asked Angelica.

Everyone looked at each other. "Let's come up with one for Angelica!" said Phil.

Angelica smirked. "Don't even try to dare me, diaper bags," she said. "There's nothing you could come up with that I can't do."

"Talk back to a growed-up?" offered Chuckie, looking to make sure there weren't any grown-ups around.

"Too easy!" Angelica scoffed.

"Climb to the tippy top of that tree?" Lil suggested.

"Try again!" Angelica said.

Just then Tommy smiled. "Angelica, I dare you to be nice to everyone all day long!"

Angelica did not like the sound of that. "That's just plain dumb," she said nervously.

Kimi joined in. "How about if we make it even more inneresting? If you can't be good all day long, you have to give us your ice-cream cone today."

Everyone gasped.

Angelica had an even better idea. "And if I *can* be nice all day, I get *your* ice-cream cones. All five of 'em." The babies nodded.

Angelica smiled pleasantly at the babies. How hard could this "being nice" thing really be?

The kids watched in surprise as Angelica took turns on the swings. She didn't tell anyone that the sandbox was actually a big box of kitty litter so she could have it all to herself. She even waited in line at the water fountain and said "please" and "thank you" to everyone.

Then the McNulty brothers arrived at the playground—Timmy, Terry, Todd, Ty, and Teddy. All they ever did was bully kids around. They buried babies' binkies in the sandbox. They stole kids' bottles and put sand in their hair. There was only one thing to do when the McNultys showed up at the playground—run!

Chuckie gulped.

"It's okay," said Tommy. "Nobody bosses Angelica around."

They looked over and saw Angelica helping a little girl tie her shoelaces. Just then Timmy McNulty came over.

"Everything but the seesaw is off-limits!" he yelled at the babies. Everyone knew Timmy McNulty hated the seesaw. It made him sick.

Angelica walked right over to Timmy. "Excuse me, I hate to interrupt," she said pleasantly, "but I was just wondering what was going on?"

Timmy told her that since she wasn't a McNulty, she could only play on the seesaw.

Angelica wrinkled her nose. "I don't mean to be rude, but you and your brothers get to go on all the good stuff, and the rest of us get to play on the stinky seesaw?"

"Yeah," said Timmy. "Wanna do somethin' about it?"

"No, thank you," Angelica said politely, and skipped away.

Tommy, Chuckie, Kimi, Phil, and Lil couldn't believe their eyes.

"Angelica!" Tommy said. "You gots to help us! You're the only one who can stand up to the bully boys!"

"I'm sorry, babies," Angelica reminded them, "but I've got a dare to keep." She smiled at them. "And 'sides, the ice-cream man will be here soon."

"But, Angelica!" Chuckie cried. "This is life or breath!"

Angelica thought for a moment. "Promise you'll never make me be nice again?"

"We promise," said Tommy. Everyone nodded.

"And you'll still give me all your ice cream?"

"Anything!" said Tommy.

"I'll do it!" said Angelica.

Angelica marched over to the McNulty brothers.

"Okay, McNulty," she growled to Timmy. "This playground isn't big enough for the two of us. It's time for you and your bully brothers to leave."

"Who's gonna make me?" said Timmy. "You and what army?"

Angelica motioned for the babies to join her. "Me and *this* army," she said.

"We're gonna play a little game called 'I Dare You.' And the winner gets to be the boss of this playground. The loser has to leave and go to the playground on the other side of the park."

"The one with the rusty swings?" asked Timmy.

"That's the one," replied Angelica.

"You're on!" Timmy said.

Angelica dared Lil and Terry to eat bugs. Lil won hands down.

Then Timmy dared Chuckie and Todd to see who could climb the highest on the monkey bars. But Chuckie was afraid of heights.

The kids were tied. It was up to Angelica to come up with a dare for her and Timmy. A huge smile spread across Angelica's face.

"I dare you to a seesaw contest!" she said.

Timmy turned pale. "That's for babies!" he said, stalling for time.

"Come on, bully boy!" Angelica taunted.

Timmy took one look at the dreaded seesaw and ran! After a minute his brothers followed right behind him.

The babies had won the game . . . and Angelica was back to her bossy self.

When the ice-cream man came, Tommy's father, Stu, brought the babies each an ice-cream cone. "Fork them over," Angelica demanded after Stu was out of earshot. Angelica got her five ice-cream cones—and a big stomachache, too!